Disney FAIRIES

Annual 2013

EGMONT

We bring stories to life

First published in Great Britain 2012
by Egmont UK Limited,
239 Kensington High Street,
London W8 6SA

Editor: Catherine Such
Art Editor: Amanda Hartley
Writer: Olivia McLearon
Designer: Aimee Gillett
Editorial Assistant: Hannah Greenfield
Group Editor: Kate Graham

© 2012 Disney Enterprises, Inc.

ISBN 978 1 4052 6329 0
51518/1
Printed in Italy

This magical annual belongs to

Write your name here.

Tinker Fairies

Tinker Talent

Tinker fairies repair the broken objects in Pixie Hollow. They can make anything look brand new.

Meet Tinker Bell

Creative Tink loves being a tinker fairy! She's always working on exciting new inventions.

Fairy Workshop

Tink works in a special workshop called Tinkers' Nook with her tinker friends, Clank and Bobble.

Jinker Bell

9

Colour
Add some fairy colours to Tink.

Tink sulks on a leaf. With nothing to tinker with, she's starting to get bored.

Nothing ever breaks round here!

But maybe there's someone who needs me ...

Tink decides to go to Lizzy's house and see if she needs anything fixing.

I see! You want some work to do!

Lizzy hurries off to her drawers. She returns with a big basket full of broken toys and objects.

Wow! I'll get straight to it!

Puzzling Fun

Use your talent to solve these teasers!

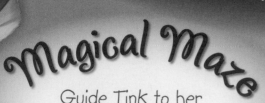

Magical Maze

Guide Tink to her workshop, collecting her tools on the way.

Finish

Start

Which Tink?

Can you work out which Tink is the odd one out?

a
b
c
d

In the Shadows

Which shadow matches this picture of Fawn exactly?

a
b
c

Answers on page 67.

Tinker Time

The fairies are busy collecting lost objects.
Can you spot five differences in the bottom picture?

Colour a bell each time you find a difference.

Answers on page 67.

Colour
Add some colour to this picture of Tink at work.

Fairy Fact
Tink's house is made out of a kettle she found on the beach.

Welcome to
Jinkers' Nook

Tinkers' Nook is where the tinker fairies work. Let's find out more about this magical place!

Fairy Mary

Fairy Mary is in charge at Tinkers' Nook. She is kind and fair, but can be strict when she needs to be!

Working Together

It's always busy at Tinkers' Nook, but the fairies work together to make sure that everything runs smoothly.

Great Inventions

The tinker fairies take things from nature to make something new! A toadstool makes a great tinker's table!

Lost and Found

Tink loves using lost things from the mainland to create something shiny and new. Tinkers' Nook is full of her finds!

Can you spot a spring hidden somewhere on these pages?

Clank and Bobble

This fun-loving pair try hard to get things right, but they don't always manage it!

Garden Fairies

Flower Fairies

Garden fairies care for plants and flowers. It's their job to paint the petals every season.

Meet Rosetta

Garden fairy Rosetta is a brilliant artist. She likes to make sure that everything in nature looks perfect.

Home Sweet Home

Garden fairies make their homes inside pretty flowers. Rosetta lives in a sweet-scented pink rose.

Colour
Use your brightest pens to colour Rosetta.

Rosetta

The Gift of Friendship

Read the story below. When you see a picture, shout out the right word.

Daisy   Bee   Rosetta   Tinker Bell

It was the day before Silvermist's arrival day and [Rosetta] wanted to make something extra-special to give to her. "[Tinker Bell] what do you think I should make?" [Rosetta] asked. [Tinker Bell] smiled and said, "Now, where's the fun if I tell you what to make?"

So, [Rosetta] sat down and started thinking and thinking ...

But an hour later, she still hadn't thought of anything!  saw her friend's troubled expression and wanted to

help. She flew over to her and said, "Look around you."

looked around at her beautiful surroundings and noticed a

. "Hello ," she said. "What are you doing?"

The was buzzing around a pretty .

"That's it!" cried. "I'll make a friendship bracelet

for Silvermist!" She thanked the .

"This will be the best arrival day present ever!" said .

"I just know Silvermist will love it!"

The End

Fairy Fun

Answer the questions dotted around the page about this fabulous fairy scene.

How many daisies can you count on these pages?

2 Which fairy is wearing a green dress?

3 What is Iridessa holding in her hand?

24

4

Can you spot four ladybirds hiding on these pages?

5

Unscramble the letters to reveul Rosetta's favourite flower:

o r e s

6

Which fairy is hiding behind the tree?

Perfect Match

Rosetta is playing with her fluttering friends.
Which two butterflies match exactly?

a

c

b

g

d

h

f

e

Answer on page 67.

Colour
Add some pretty colours to Rosetta and the flower.

Fairy Fact
Rosetta's favourite dress is made out of rose petals.

27

Garden Friends

The gardens of Pixie Hollow are filled with some amazing animal friends.

Lovely Ladybirds

Colourful ladybirds can be spotted on plants and leaves. You have to look closely, though, because they're very small!

Beautiful Butterflies

Butterflies carry pollen from one plant to another, which helps new flowers grow.

28

Buzzy Bees

Bees are insects that produce tasty honey. But be careful around them, as they can sting!

Help the garden fairies by painting a pretty pattern on this butterfly.

Magical Magpies

Cheeky magpies can't resist sparkly objects! If they spot anything shiny, they take it and hide it in their nest!

Flower Search

Can you find these garden words hidden in the wordsearch?

J	W	J	H	P	B	O	I	A
B	U	T	T	E	R	F	L	Y
E	F	U	D	T	T	B	P	H
E	B	L	L	A	H	M	U	D
M	I	I	C	L	W	D	F	A
P	O	P	P	Y	Q	L	W	I
D	A	F	F	O	D	I	L	S
K	F	Q	W	I	U	I	Q	Y
A	R	O	S	E	S	T	N	X

ROSE   DAISY   DAFFODIL
BEE   BUTTERFLY   TULIP
PETAL   POPPY

Answers on page 67.

Fairy Pairs

Follow the pretty trails to match each fairy to her flower.

Rosetta

Tinker Bell

Fawn

Iridessa

Tigerlily

Sunflower

Rose

Daisy

Answers on page 67.

Animal Fairies

Friendly Fairies

Animal fairies look after the animals of Pixie Hollow. They can speak to them in their own language.

Meet Fawn

Animal fairy Fawn is kind and patient. She has lots of energy and is always on the move!

Animal Magic

The animal fairies paint the pretty patterns on butterflies and the dots on ladybirds!

Colour
Use your brightest pens to colour Fawn.

Fawn

33

The Popular Poppy

Stop that! The Mainland is full of flowers!

Why don't you look for another flower?

BZZZ! BZZZ

There's a field on the Mainland where only one *beautiful* poppy has grown, and all the *bees* are fighting over it.

But the bee isn't happy at being told what to do!

BZZZ!!!

BZZZZZ!!! BZZZ!

Whilst the bees continue to fight, Fawn comes up with a plan.

Flu-uit!

Fawn whistles loudly so that her fairy friends will hear.

Did you call us?

Yes! I need your help!

BZZZ! BZZZ!

Fawn shows the fairies the two bees fighting over the poppy.

Psst, psst!

But, she has a great idea! The fairies gather round to listen.

35

Vidia flies to the poppy and takes out some seeds. The bees stop and stare.

Rosetta then plants the seeds in some nice soft soil.

Plink

Plink

Silvermist sprinkles a little water over them.

And finally, Iridessa makes the sun shine brightly.

A few minutes later, the seeds begin to grow.

36

Animal Cuties

Can you work out which animal is shown in each of the close-ups below?

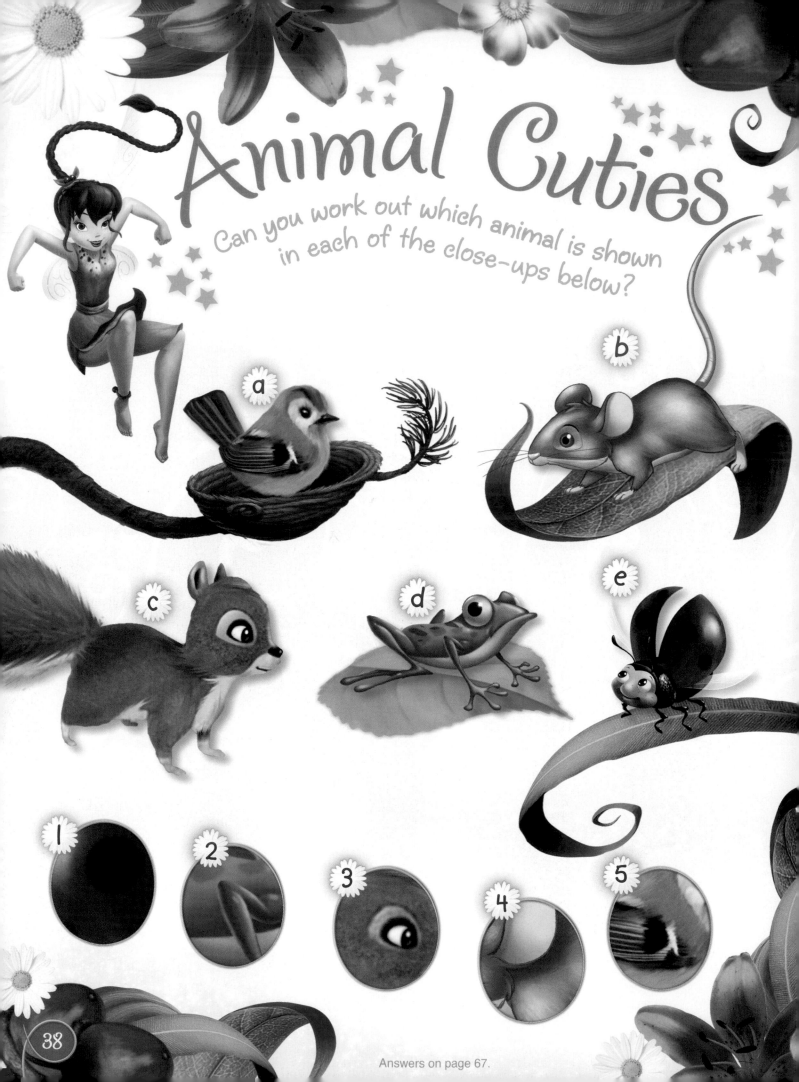

a

b

c

d

e

1

2

3

4

5

38

Colour
Add some fairy colours to this picture of Fawn.

Fairy Fact
Fawn calls her animal friends 'fuzzies'!

Fun with Fawn!

Can you help solve these magical puzzles?

Animal Changes

Cheese is taking the fairies for a ride! Can you spot five changes in picture b?

a

b

Berry Fun!

Count how many juicy berries Fawn has picked for her animal friends. 9

Friends Forever

Use the clues to match each animal to its fairy friend.

The squirrel's fairy friend has a long plait.

The mouse's fairy friend has blonde hair.

The butterfly's fairy friend is wearing a pink dress.

The frog's fairy friend has long black hair.

The firefly's fairy friend is wearing a yellow dress

Answers on page 67.

41

Special Friends

Let's meet Cheese and Blaze, Fawn and Tink's special animal friends ...

Cheese the Mouse

Cheese is a very faithful friend. He loves chatting with Fawn and is always happy to listen to Tink's problems.

Fantastic Friend

Shy Cheese likes to help his friends whenever he can. He pulls the heavy cart the fairies use to make deliveries.

Blaze the Firefly

Blaze and Tink have a special bond. His bright flashing light is very useful, and Blaze is also a helpful friend to Iridessa.

Friends Forever

Tink and Blaze weren't always great friends! When they first met, Blaze ate Tink's lunch and she wasn't very happy!

Can you find five bird's eggs hidden on these pages?

Light Fairies

Magical Talent

Light fairies work with their water fairy friends to make pretty rainbows appear!

Meet Iridessa

Light fairy Iridessa is sensible and loyal. She is always happy and has a sunny smile.

Firefly Friends

It's the light fairies' job to give fireflies their spark so they glow brightly at night.

Iridessa

Colour
Make Iridessa glow with your brightest pens.

45

Helpful Fairies

Write your name in the spaces then read your special fairy story.

It was a beautiful spring day in Pixie Hollow and almost time for Iridessa to produce her first rainbow of the year.

Silvermist was all set to help – water-talent fairies are always needed for rainbow-making!

.... and Tinker Bell were really excited. They couldn't
Write your name here

wait to see the beautiful colours light up the sky.

But there was just one small problem. The rainbow wasn't in its tube!

"Oh no," exclaimed Iridessa. "Where has my rainbow gone?"

"Don't worry," .... said.
Write your name here

"With Tink's talent for fixing things,

46

I'm sure we'll think

of a way of fixing your problem."

Iridessa was thankful to her friends, but felt disappointed that

she and Silvermist couldn't manage to create a rainbow on their own.

"That's it!" Tinker Bell suddenly exclaimed. "We'll get all of the fairies

to form a rainbow in the sky, with all of their different colours!"

"What a wonderful idea," .... replied. So they told
                          Write your name here

Iridessa Tink's plan. She thought it was great and Silvermist agreed!

The fairies formed the perfect rainbow, flying through sky.

Iridessa realised the most wonderful things happen when you

work as a team and that she was very lucky

to have ....
        Write your name here

and all the other fairies as her friends.

The End

47

Magic Code

Iridessa has written a secret message.
Use the key to work out what it says.

Key:

y e i a f r

n d s o v

Iridessa's message is:

F a i r y   f r i e n d s

f o r e v e r

Answer on page 67.

Light Show

Iridessa has made a sunbeam. Can you spot five differences in the bottom picture?

Answers on page 68.

Colour a sunflower each time you spot a difference.

49

Finding Rainbows

Help Iridessa find the rainbow and reach the finish.

Make sure you collect the sunbeams on the way!

Start

Finish

Answer on page 68.

Fairy Fact

Iridessa's yellow dress is made out of sunflower petals.

Colour

Add some colour to pretty Iridessa.

Fairy Puzzles

Add a sprinkling of pixie dust to help you work out the answers to these fairy puzzles!

Join the Dots

Join the dots to find out who Iridessa has been playing with.

Odd One Out

Which of these fairies is the odd one out and why? The clue is in their talent.

a

b

c

Talent Trails
Follow the trails to match each
fairy to her talent symbol!

Rosetta

Tinker Bell

Fawn

Iridessa

Silvermist

Water globe

Sunbeam

Flower

Hammer

Bird's egg

Answers on page 68.

Water Fairies

Special Talent

Water fairies create ripples in streams and sprinkle flowers with water.

Meet Silvermist

Water fairy Silvermist is calm and gentle. She's always there for her friends.

Helping Hand

Water fairies carry water droplets to the birds and animals of Pixie Hollow.

Colour
Add some sparkling colours to Silvermist.

Silvermist

A Secret to Share

It's just stopped raining in Pixie Hollow. The fairies have come out to play.

I love the scent of damp fields!

But Rosetta isn't happy!

Look what the weather's done to my hair!

Dampness makes my hair go frizzy!

Suddenly, Silvermist spots something.

A pretty flower has been splattered with muddy rain water.

Silvermist wants to clean the poor flower up and asks Rosetta to help.

But Rosetta doesn't want to because the mud is dirty!

Silvermist is annoyed at the garden fairy. But Rosetta has another idea.

Don't worry! I have a secret plan.

Rosetta flies into the air, sprinkling pixie dust around the muddy flower.

What are you doing?

Silvermist is amazed as Rosetta works her special magic.

In no time at all, the pretty flower is blooming once more. Rosetta boasts that she has cleaned the flower without getting dirty!

You were flitterific!

But suddenly, Rosetta gets a shock. ...

Eek!

Mirror Message

Silvermist has written a secret message for you.

1 Hold this page up to a mirror to reveal the message.

What is your special fairy talent?

2 Write your answer to Silvermist's question in the space below.

3 Write your own mirror message for Silvermist!

Answer on page 68.

60

Colour
Add some fairy colours to Silvermist.

Fairy Fact
Silvermist's house has dewdrops for windows.

Magical Puzzles

Make a splash and help Silvermist solve these watery teasers!

Pond Puzzler

How many of each of the creatures below can you count in the pond?

Pretty Word

Cross out the letters that appear twice then write the remaining letters below to reveal a colourful word.

rsaimnpbposwm

_ _ _ _ _ _ _

Which Way?

Which trail should Silvermist take to find her water globe?

a

b

c

Answers on page 68.

Missing Pieces

Which jigsaw pieces complete this picture
of Silvermist and Tinker Bell?

a

b

c

d

Answers on page 68.

What's your Fairy Talent?

Circle your answers to discover your fairy talent.

1 You absolutely adore ...

a Animals
b Flowers
c Making things

2 You are known for being ...

a Fun
b Sweet
c Loyal

3 Your favourite colour is ...

a Red
b Pink
c Green

4 Your favourite animal is ...

a A mouse
b A butterfly
c A firefly

5 You don't like it when ...

a People are too serious
b You have to play indoors
c You can't fix something

Turn the page to reveal your fairy talent ...

... continued from page 65

Mostly As

Being an animal fairy, like Fawn, is the perfect talent for a fun, playful character like you!

Mostly Bs

You love pretty things and the great outdoors, just like Rosetta. You are a garden fairy.

Mostly Cs

Like Tink, you're creative and love to make things. You would be a great tinker fairy!

Answers

Pages 14-15 Puzzling Fun

Magical Maze

Which Tink?
Tink c is the odd one out.

In the Shadows
Shadow c matches Fawn.

Page 16 Tinker Time

Pages 24-25 Fairy Fun

1. Three daisies.
2. Tinker Bell.
3. A flower.
5. Rose.
6. Vidia.

Page 26 Perfect Match

Butterflies a and d match.

Page 30 Flower Search

Page 31 Fairy Pairs

Rosetta - Rose.

Tinker Bell - Daisy.

Fawn - Tigerlily.

Iridessa - Sunflower.

Page 38 Animal Cuties

1 - e.

2 - d.

3 - c.

4 - b.

5 - a.

Pages 40-41 Fun with Fawn!

Berry Fun
Fawn has gathered nine berries.

Friends Forever
Squirrel – Fawn.
Mouse – Tink.
Butterfly – Rosetta.
Frog – Silvermist.
Firefly – Iridessa.

Page 48 Magic Code

Fairy friends forever.

Answers

Page 49 — Light Show

Pages 52-53 — Fairy Puzzles

Join the Dots
Iridessa has been playing with a butterfly.

Odd One Out
Rosetta, b, is the odd one out – the others are tinker fairies.

Talent Trails
Rosetta – flower.
Tink – hammer.
Fawn – bird's egg.
Iridessa – sunbeam.
Silvermist – water globe.

Pages 62-63 — Magical Puzzles

Pond Puzzler
Fish - 2.
Bug - 5.
Butterfly - 3.
Frog - 2.

Pretty Word
Rainbow.

Which Way?
Path a leads to Silvermist's globe.

Pages 50 — Finding Rainbows

Page 60 — Mirror Message

What is your special fairy talent?

Page 64 — Missing Pieces

Pieces a, b and c complete the picture.

We hope you enjoyed your fairies annual!